WOMEN'S PROFESSIONAL BASKETBALL

Teamwork:

The
CLEVELAND ROCKERS

in Action

Thomas S. Owens
Diana Star Helmer

The Rosen Publishing Group's
PowerKids Press™
New York

To everyone who has waited or worked for a dream. Here's proof that dreams come true.

Published in 1999 by The Rosen Publishing Group, Inc.
29 East 21st Street, New York, NY 10010

First Edition

Book Design: Michael de Guzman

Photo Credits: p. 4 © Nathaniel Butler/WNBA Enterprises, LLC; p. 5 © Bill Baptist/WNBA Enterprises, LLC; p. 7 © Reuters/Sersgio Moraes/Archive Photos; p. 8 © Glenn Edwards/WNBA Enterprises, LLC; p. 11 © Bill Baptist/WNBA Enterprises, LLC (inset) © Allsport/NBA Photos; pp. 12, 16, 19, 20, 21 © Greg Shamus/WNBA Enterprises, LLC; p. 15 © Norman Trotman/WNBA Enterprises, LLC.

Owens, Tom, 1960-
    Teamwork: the Cleveland Rockers in action / by Thomas S. Owens and Diana Star Helmer.
        p.   cm. — (Women's professional basketball)
    Includes index.
    Summary: Profiles some of the key players on the Cleveland Rockers and describes the team's first year in the WNBA.
    ISBN 0-8239-5241-X
    1. Cleveland Rockers (Basketball team)—Juvenile literature. 2. Basketball for women—United States—Juvenile literature.
[1. Cleveland Rockers (Basketball team.) 2. Women basketball players. 3. Basketball players.] I. Helmer, Diana Star, 1962-
II. Title. III. Series: Owens, Tom, 1960-   Women's professional basketball.
GV885.52.C57094 1998
796.323'64'0977132—dc21   98-5640
                                                                                                                      CIP
                                                                                                                      AC

Manufactured in the United States of America

Contents

Rock On

The Cleveland Rockers had just beat a tough team. Now they needed two more wins to make the **play-offs** (PLAY-offs). Next they met the New York Liberty, who'd already won a spot in the play-offs. The Rockers played hard. But with just eight seconds left to play, they were still two points behind. With one last chance, Rocker Michelle Edwards threw the ball. Swish! She got a three-pointer, and Cleveland won! If they could beat New York one more time, Cleveland would be in the first-ever WNBA play-offs.

◁ The Rockers worked really hard to win a spot in the play-offs.

5

Sisters of the NBA

The National Basketball Association (NBA), which is the men's basketball **league** (LEEG), started the Women's National Basketball Association (WNBA). The NBA decided that the women's teams would play in cities where the men's teams played. The WNBA would play while the NBA was on summer vacation.

The idea for the WNBA began in 1996 when the Olympics were held in the United States. The whole world watched as the U.S. Women's Basketball Team won the gold medal. The American people wanted to be able to see these new basketball stars play in their own league in the United States. One of the first eight WNBA teams would be in Cleveland, Ohio.

Many of the players on the 1996 gold-medal Olympic team, such as Sheryl Swoopes (middle left) and Lisa Leslie (middle right) now play in the WNBA. They are shown here with Olympic teammates Jennifer Azzi (far left) and Venus Lacey (far right).

Play Loud and Long

Cleveland is home to many sports. The Cleveland Cavaliers play NBA basketball. The Cleveland Indians play major league baseball. Cleveland is also famous because it is home to the Rock and Roll Hall of Fame and Museum. Music fans go there to learn about the stars and history of rock and roll. That's why Cleveland's WNBA team was named the Rockers. The team's **logo** (LOH-goh) shows the letter "R" shaped like an electric guitar. The team wanted their fans to feel like dancing when they watched them play!

◁ The Rockers' logo shows that they're proud to play for Cleveland.

Start with a Star

Lynette Woodard always loved basketball. Her uncle, Hubert "Geese" Aubie, was one of the famous Harlem Globetrotters. The Globetrotters didn't play basketball to win—they put on a basketball show! Lynette wanted to do that too. But the Globetrotters had always been just for men.

Lynette played basketball in college. She scored more points than any woman ever had scored before. She even won an Olympic gold medal in 1984. And the next year, she became the first woman Globetrotter! "It was like having ten big brothers," Lynette says of the Globetrotters.

Lynette was 37 when she joined the Rockers. She felt like the team's big sister.

Not only did Lynette get to be the first woman on the Globetrotters, but she got to be one of the players in the first WNBA season too! ▷

A New World for Basketball

For years the United States had no **professional** (proh-FEH-shuh-nul) women's basketball teams. Lynette Woodard had to go to Italy and Japan to play for money and prizes. Even though Europe had professional teams, it didn't have college teams. Isabelle Fijalkowski left France in 1994 so she could play college basketball in the United States. Afterward, she returned to Europe to play professional basketball.

But the WNBA changed women's basketball. Isabelle Fijalkowski and teammate Eva Nemcova left Europe to play professional basketball in Cleveland. Isabelle helped Eva learn English.

◁ Before the WNBA, American women had to go to Europe to play professional basketball. But now European women are coming to the United States to play.

13

No Place Like Home

Rocker Janice Lawrence Braxton used to play professional basketball in Italy. She enjoyed it, but it wasn't always easy. Sometimes her Italian team couldn't practice because cows got to the field first! And sometimes the gyms where they wanted to play had cracked floors. But Janice says, "I've been able to travel to places I never would have gone. And I've met people I'll remember for a lifetime." She even met her husband in Europe. But Janice's first Rockers game was extra special to her. "For the first time in fourteen years, my mother got to watch me play basketball," Janice says.

Being able to play professional basketball in her own country is very important to Janice. ▷

Soul Sisters

Rocker Jenny Boucek was always tired when her team played the Utah Starzz. That's because she and Starzz player Wendy Palmer would stay up all night talking before the game! The two players are best friends who met in college. Jenny says, "We're so different on the outside. Besides basketball, we do different things with different people." But these two players are close on the inside. "We call each other soul sisters," says Jenny. "Family doesn't have anything to do with being alike. We'll always be soul sisters."

◁ Even though Jenny and Wendy play on different teams, they are still best friends.

17

Fun for Fans

Fans are important members of every sports team. The Rockers understand this, so they keep ticket prices low so that more fans can come to the games. Groups like the Boys and Girls Clubs of America get free tickets. The Rockers sometimes let fans watch practices, or they teach kids how to play basketball. And Rockers always meet their fans after home games. At half-time, the Rockers have contests just for kids or contests for **charity** (CHAR-uh-tee). One night more than 300 Girl Scouts came to see a game. Then they had a sleep-over at the arena!

Young fans are very special to the Rockers. ▷

Teamwork off the Court

After only three games, Rocker Michelle Edwards hurt her knee. She couldn't play for eight games. The Rockers won only two games without her. Michelle didn't like to see her team lose, so she carefully watched her team play. She saw what her team needed to do. When Michelle got better, she showed her team what she thought they needed to do to win. The Rockers went on to win eight games in a row. It was the longest winning streak in WNBA history. "I'm not the only reason we won," Michelle says. "But I knew I could make a difference."

◁ Sometimes someone can help a team improve by taking a break and watching the game.

Rolling On

The Rockers' first year had a rocky start. But with teamwork, they finished with fifteen wins and thirteen losses. Eva Nemcova led the WNBA in three-point shots. Isabelle Fijalkowski was second in the league in **field goals** (FEELD GOHLZ). Janice Braxton was third in the league in **rebounds** (REE-bowndz). After the first season, some Rockers went to Europe to play professionally. Some took other jobs. But they all look forward to playing again. The WNBA is planning new teams in Washington DC and Detroit. And there will be more games each season. That means that the Rockers will have more chances to earn a spot in the play-offs.

Web Sites:

You can learn more about women's professional basketball at these Web sites:

http://www.wnba.com
http://www.fullcourt.com

Glossary

charity (CHAR-uh-tee) An act that helps people who are in need.

field goal (FEELD GOHL) When a ball goes through the hoop for two points.

league (LEEG) A group of teams that play against each other in the same sport.

logo (LOH-goh) A picture that stands for a team's name.

play-off (PLAY-off) Games played by the best teams after the regular season ends to see who will play in the championship game.

professional (proh-FEH-shuh-nul) An athlete who gets paid to play a sport.

rebound (REE-bownd) When you get control of the ball after a missed shot.

Index